For Cécile

Copyright © 1994 by Nord-Süd Verlag AG, Gossau Zürich, Switzerland
First published in Switzerland under the title *Martin hat keine Angst mehr*
English translation copyright © 1994 by North-South Books Inc.

First published in the United States, Great Britain, Canada,
Australia, and New Zealand in 1994 by North-South Books,
an imprint of Nord-Süd Verlag AG, Gossau Zürich, Switzerland.

Distributed in the United States by North-South Books Inc., New York.

Library of Congress Cataloging-in-Publication Data is available.
A CIP catalogue record for this book is available from The British Library.
ISBN 1-55858-267-3 (trade binding)   ISBN 1-55858-268-1 (library binding)

1 3 5 7 9 10 8 6 4 2
Printed in Belgium

Ingrid Ostheeren

Martin and
the Pumpkin Ghost

Illustrated by Christa Unzner-Fischer

TRANSLATED AND ADAPTED BY J. ALISON JAMES

North-South Books

New York

Martin was scared of *everything*. Not just wasps and spiders and monsters in the dark, but dogs and bullies and the teacher, and even his sister Clara. He was so scared, he had nightmares about being scared.

Then one night he had a dream. It was a crazy dream, and he laughed when he remembered it. But it stuck with him and he began to wonder if it might be real.

In the dream a witch—a good witch—said to him, "Ma-a-artin…don't be afra-a-aid. Listen to the pumpkin gho-o-ost."

"P-p-pumpkin ghost?" Martin stammered, afraid as usual.

"A ki-i-ind ghost. He will help you be bra-a-ave."

When he woke up, he lay in bed a long time wondering if the dream could be true.

Suddenly his big sister came in and pulled down the covers. "Get up, you lazy bones!" she shouted. "You'll be late for school!"

Martin heard a little voice: *Be ni-i-ice to your sister.*

It took him by surprise, and he found himself saying, "Good morning, Clara," in a cheerful voice.

She looked at him, surprised, and said, "Good morning, Martin." It was the first friendly thing she'd said to him in weeks.

At school Martin unpacked his books. Oh, no! He'd left his homework on the kitchen table. His teacher would kill him. Martin would probably even have to stay after school and do it all over again.

Tell the teacher, Ma-a-artin.

Yikes! That voice again. Was it a pumpkin ghost? Martin waved his hand through the air to try and catch the ghost.

"Yes, Martin?" The teacher thought he had a question.

"I—um—I left my homework at home."

The teacher raised his eyebrows. "Well, it's refreshing to have such honesty. Just bring it in tomorrow, and don't forget."

"Thank you, pumpkin ghost!" Martin thought.

Martin went outside to eat his lunch. Some older kids were playing a game. Just as Martin got out his sandwich, a big boy barged right into him. The sandwich fell to the ground.

Martin was nearly in tears. He hated bullies! He wanted to hit the boy, but the boy was so much bigger.

Wa-a-ait, Martin, cautioned a voice in his ear.

"Sorry about that," the older boy said. He picked up Martin's sandwich and brushed it off. "I hope it's still all right to eat."

Martin nodded, astonished. That ghost pumpkin sure is powerful, he thought.

Martin walked home with his friend Hanna. They were laughing and talking when they saw that Mr. Fisher's dog was out. It was barking and growling at them.

"Oh, no!" Hanna said. She stopped short. The dog bared his teeth and snarled. Martin saw that a dog that size could easily jump the fence. He was terrified and couldn't move.

Keep walking. Look stra-a-aight ahead. Don't be afra-a-aid.

"Let's keep walking," Martin said quietly to Hanna. "Look straight ahead and pretend you're not afraid."

As they calmly walked past the fence, the dog stopped barking.

Martin was so excited, he nearly gave away his secret. "That pumpkin ghost is always right," he said.

"Pumpkin ghost?" asked Hanna.

"It's just an expression," Martin said quickly. "It helps me to be brave."

"Well, whatever it is, it worked," Hanna said cheerfully.

That afternoon Martin was shooting goals against the garage door. Every time he scored, he yelled, "Goal!" He was feeling great. Then he kicked the ball and it sailed in a high arc over the fence. He heard a crash and a clatter in Mrs. Singer's garden.

His ball had knocked over a flower-pot, and the pot had shattered.

"Goal," Martin muttered mournfully.

He didn't need the pumpkin ghost to tell him what to do. One time he had broken Mrs. Singer's window and tried to run away. But she had caught him, and then he'd been in big trouble.

He rang Mrs. Singer's bell.

"I'm really sorry," he said. "I'll buy you a new one with my allowance.
And I'll put the plant back in."

"Don't be silly," Mrs. Singer said. "I have lots of pots. But I could use
some help replanting the geranium."

Martin went down to the pond. His secret place to hide and think was in an old sycamore tree. Someday he would build a tree house up there, right over the water.

But something was not right. Someone was sitting in his tree. When Martin got closer, he saw it was Peter, the biggest bully in his class.

Martin was so angry, he didn't stop to think. He didn't even have time to be scared. He went at Peter like a whirlwind and pulled him from the tree. "Get out of here!" he shouted.

"You don't own that tree," Peter said.

Tell him about the tree-e-e house.

"No way! I'm not telling," Martin said out loud.

"What?" asked Peter.

"I'm not talking to you," said Martin.

Go-o-o on, tell him!

The pumpkin ghost hadn't been wrong yet. But to tell his most secret idea to his worst enemy—it was crazy.

"What are you not telling?" Peter demanded.

"Um," Martin stalled. Then he drew in a breath and said, "Isn't this a great tree for a tree house?"

Peter smiled. "I don't know. Let's test it out." He scrambled up the tree. Martin was right on his heels.

Peter leaned out over the water. "It's perfect," he said. "I can get some tools and some nails."

"I've been saving wood," Martin said.

They walked home together. As they were crossing the bridge, Martin heard the little voice: *See you la-a-ater, kid!* A whooshing sound swept past his ear and under the bridge. He heard a splash and a light-hearted laugh.

"Did you drop something?" Peter asked.
Martin grinned. "Nah, it was just the pumpkin ghost."
"Pumpkin ghost! You really are nuts, you know."
"I know," said Martin happily.
The two new friends went off together down the road.